COSMIC LOVE

poems + prayers to my future lover

by Rachel White

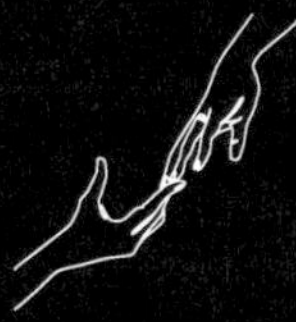

Dear future lover,

Take my poems and prayers as devotional
offerings to our love... Love that spans across
time and space, I know we will cross paths in
divine timing. The blank pages are for you
to write your own words of love back to me.

With love,
Your future lover

I find myself awake, in a fantasy of our love

I follow the yearning in, the dripping void of

I sense you reaching now, breaking the rules
of space and time

It feels different when you are here, like all
the colours suddenly rhyme

May you feel purpose in your journey
May joy be your days laced
May you feel complete within yourself
May you feel the presence of my grace
May you love fully and deeply
but not as completely as you will with me
May you clear the space needed
that together for us to be

Sometimes I wonder if I am enough
For how I imagine the embrace of your love
Will I appear as what you expected to see
Am I everything you long for your lover to be
I imagine you telling me to you I am perfect
From when we have wrinkles to back when
we first met

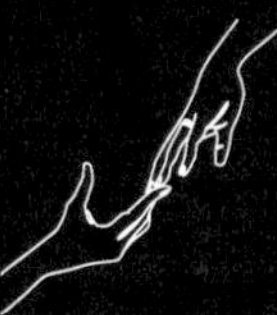

Oh my lover, all the thing I will do
when the time does come that I get to meet
you....

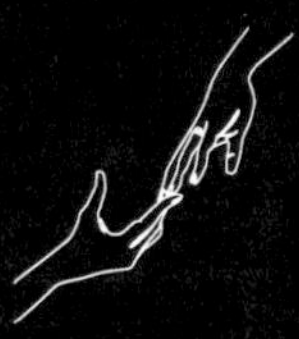

Our story is written, it is already so
In our space apart our love still did grow
In the fabric of the cosmos our love does
exist
From the moment we were born to the
moment we first kissed
The story is written, for us to soon play our
part
In our story we have been living back to the
very start
All along in our adventures, you were tied to
me
There was no other way for us to find each
other sooner, you will soon see

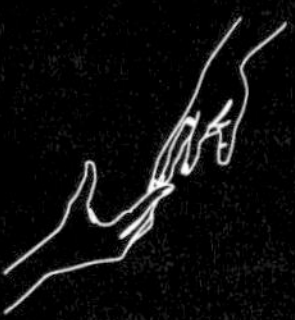

Sometimes I imagine that my hand touching
me
belongs to you my lover, tracing my body
slowly

My love I pour into you
I believe in your vision
I support you fully
In living your mission

I hope you think about me
As much as I you
If not yet
You will do soon

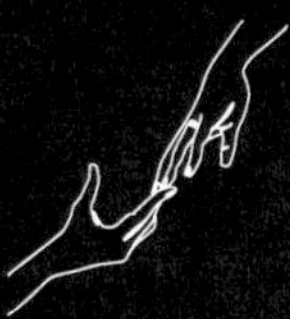

May you stand in your presence
While I dance for you
May your gaze never leave me
To me it looks right through
Piercing into the deepest depths
You see all of my longing
In union together
A perfect belonging

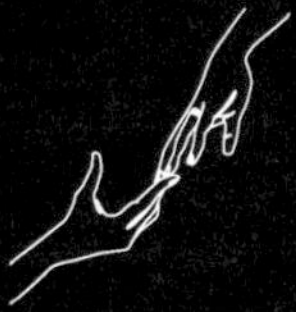

I am an infinite versions of me
I hope you love each of us equally

May your life fall apart
at least once in your story
so you learn how to pick up the pieces
and let go of your worry
may you have your heart broken
so you know how to heal
may your entire reality shatter
so after the storm you know what is real
may life itself prepare you
for cosmic union with me
we shall weather any storm together
no matter how big it seems
may you know how to stay grounded
in the eye of all the mess
to hear the coherence of our love be
stronger
to feel that we are blessed

We break the laws of the universe
even when it's an inside joke between us
the rules of life do not hold any power
when face to face with our love

Oh your gorgeous smile
it takes me to different places
new worlds and new dimensions
while my heart beats and races

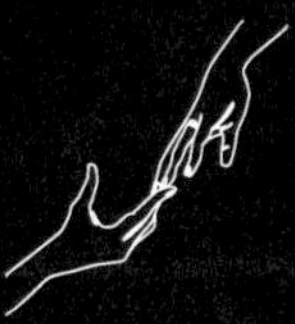

You are the sun to my moon
the sand to my sea, the tree to my wind
together we fit harmoniously

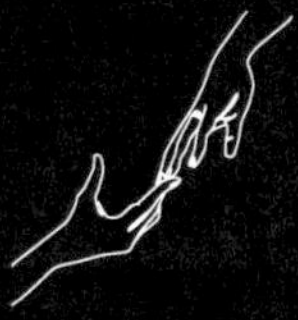

Our most boring days will be made magic
the most mundane of tasks will be ecstatic

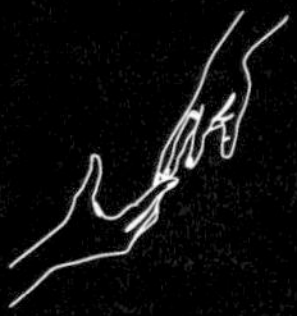

I solemnly swear with you to be honest
I devotionally declare to keep this promise

You should know that I can get a little
impatient, and I have a tendency towards
anxious isolation. Sometimes I feel so restless
and feel nothing but agitation. But I will call
on your love to soften, sometimes I just need
space, even when I get like this next to me
you will always have a place.

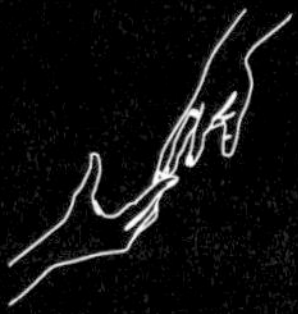

Yes.

You got me thinking empty
nothing in my brain
you got me stumped for words
nothing at all to say
you got me fully present
completely lost in you
nothing makes sense
nothing at all to do...

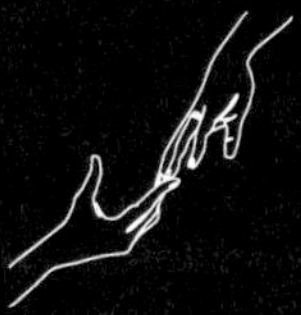

I can't wait for the days that I get
to wake up next to you
to roll over and see your face
to indulge in that view

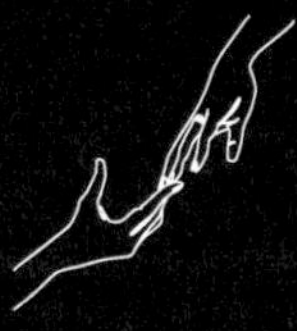

Together we will start a new legacy
a new lineage to ripple through time
we will build and nurture our empire
it will be epic and sublime
with love our closest we hold
until we do grow old
our lives will be full of great stories
through our lineage they will be told

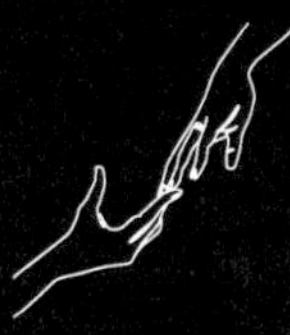

I cannot promise I that will always be sweet
or nice, or soft spoken
I cannot promise that nothing we create
will ever end up broken
I cannot promise that I will not get jealous
or anxious or annoyed
I cannot promise that there will not be some
things I may try to avoid

What I can promise is to allow you to see
all of me, piece by piece in all my glory
to peel back layers to get to the core
the light and dark of me you will explore

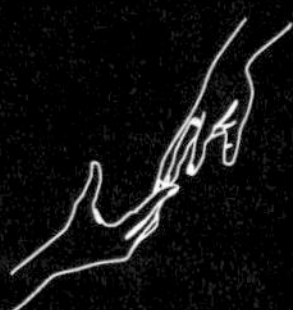

Ti amo
Je t'aime
Volim te
Eu te amo
Te iubesc
Wǒ ài nǐ
Saya sayang awak
I love you

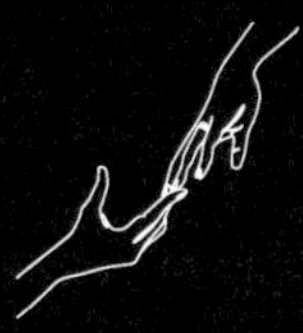

I imagine us in our kitchen slow dancing
I imagine turning around to see you there
standing
I imagine you provoking me to play
I imagine being with you all through the day
I imagine you sharing your interests with me
I imagine me listening to you excitedly
I imagine us travelling together
I imagine us exploring in every weather
I imagine with you a sense of peace
I imagine my love for you will only increase
I imagine us staying up so late
I imagine us so grateful that together we
meet our fate
I imagine you telling me that you love me
I imagine all these things endlessly

My words could never be enough
to completely capture the feeling of my love
but take them anyway as they are
for you future lover I know you are not far

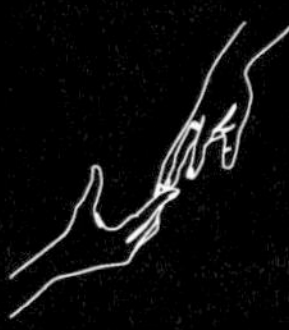

I vow to love you completely while we dive
head first into our love story

I vow that my love will be so loud that you
can hear it even when the world is silent,
and so bright that you can see it even when
the lights are out

I vow to save you a seat at every table and
to laugh at all the dirty jokes you save just
for me

I vow to create secret moments with you in
crowed rooms

I vow to be the kind of trouble you are so
glad walked into your life

I vow to keep sacred our lavender haze for
all my days